Dr. Z's Menagerie #2

Written by
JERRY ZUCKERMAN

Illustrated by
JAMES SIEGFRIED

Dr. Z's Menagerie
Published by Jerry Zuckerman
For more information visit
www.drzmenagerie.com

ISBN: 978-0-6922827-0-0

Text copyright © 2014 by Jerry Zuckerman

Illustrations copyright © 2014 by James Siegfried

Cover design and illustrations by Jim Siegfried
Interior layout and production by Gary A Rosenberg • www.thebookcouple.com

Printed in the United States of America

Introduction

Dr. Z is a wonderful, whimsical character. With degrees in veterinary science and psychology, he solves a multitude of problems in the animal kingdom.

In the second of the Dr. Z's Menagerie books, Dr. Z continues to solve the unusual problems of various animals. With clever rhymes and imaginative solutions, he once again comes to their rescue.

Dr. Z's solutions are certainly unique, as you will see in the stories within.

Cheetah Joe

There once was a cheetah
    named Joe
Who ran exceedingly slow.
And since he could barely run
The other cheetahs made fun.

1

He had no get up and go
When chasing down the prey.
In motion he was slow
And they always got away.

As a result he was often depressed
And under a great deal of stress.
When you don't bring home the dinner
You don't feel much like a winner.

Nan was the wife of Joe the cheetah.
And never there was a wife any sweeter.

Someone had to come up with a plan.
And the someone who did was someone
    named Nan.

For Joe had become an insufferable cynic.
The effect was plain to see.

So Nan took Joe to a special clinic
Run by Dr. Z.

Dr. Z did an MRI
And found the answer on the very first try.

8

He found a chip upon Joe's shoulders.
It weighed on him like a ton of boulders.

9

Zapping the chip was very simple.
And Joe never once said "Ouch."

All that was left was a tiny dimple.
And his shoulders no longer slouched.

Joe was released by Dr. Z.
Having made a full recovery.

Joe walked out into the sun.
And then slow Joe did run, run, run!

Bloodhound Kent

There once was a bloodhound
   named Kent
Who couldn't pick up a scent.

When the other hounds would
   hunt for foxes
Kent would hunt for tissue boxes.

Did he have a cold or perhaps the flu?
He really didn't have a clue.
So Kent was sent to Dr. Z
To test his nose for allergies.

There was another hound named Basil
Who had an overly sensitive nasal.
His sense of smell was way too strong.
He felt there must be something wrong.

He too was sent to Dr. Z
To rid him of this malady.
So both arrived, but with different issues.
Kent was the one with the box of tissues.

19

Dr. Z came on the scene
And he hooked them up to a strange machine.

Next he turned the switch.
They both began to twitch.

21

And before it could be stopped
DNA had been swapped.

Kent went on his merry way
With his brand new DNA.
He smelled the roses in
   the park.
Then found a tree and
   made his mark.

As to the effect on our friend Basil
Here is Dr. Z's appraisal.
"Basil still can smell the flowers.
However, with diminished power."

In they had come with opposite scents.
Two distressed hounds named Basil and Kent.
And out they went with no more trouble.
Basil smelled less and Kent smelled double.

Eagle Tim

Everyone knows if you're a bald eagle
Having a head of hair is illegal.
But there was an eagle named Tim.
And that didn't matter to him.

Tim was an eagle with a full head of hair.
And he told the others he just didn't care.
The other eagles were appalled.
Tim was the only eagle not bald.

They demanded he cut his hair.
Or else he would be banished.
It was more than he could bear.
And one day he just vanished.

Tim had taken to the sky.
And in this atmospheric zone
Nobody could hear him cry.
For Tim was truly all alone.

Under all this mental stress
Tim could tell he was depressed.
So he made a date with Dr. Z.
An expert in animal psychology.

Dr. Z ran a bunch of tests
To find out why he was depressed.
He even used hypnosis
To reach his diagnosis.

By playing tricky mental games
He figured out what was to blame.
There was one thing wrong and one thing only.
Tim was just extremely lonely.

Dr. Z said, "Don't you worry.
I have the answer to your prayer."
Tim responded, "Please, Doc, hurry.
Put an end to my despair."

Dr. Z searched low and high.
He scoured every inch of sky.
He finally achieved his goal.
He found an eagle with a kindred soul.

He introduced Tim to a female eagle.
She went by the name of Kim.
And her head of hair was just as illegal.
But that didn't matter to Tim.

Dr. Z said, "Now you're cured."
It was the best news they had heard.
He made them promise then and there
That they would never cut their hair.

37

They made another vow that day.
To be together come what may.

When Dr. Z said goodbye
He had a twinkle in his eye.

38

He said, "I have a simple creed.
To help all those in time of need.
To me no creature is a freak.
Instead be proud you are unique."

The End

About the Author

Jerry Zuckerman is the creator and author of Dr. Z. In his youth, Jerry was a racquetball pro and now works as a financial advisor. *Dr. Z's Menagerie #2* is the second book in the Dr. Z series. Jerry lives in St. Louis with his wife, Linda, and dog, Spike.

About the Illustrator

James Siegfried is the illustrator of the Dr. Z series. His imagination and sense of humor is showcased on every page he illustrates. Jim also lives in St. Louis with his family and has been drawing, illustrating, and painting for most of his life.

Made in the USA
Monee, IL
27 October 2022

16625284R00029